THE THING YOU'RE GOOD AT

THE THING YOU'RE GOOD AT

Lesley Choyce

orca soundings

ORCA BOOK PUBLISHERS

Library and Archives Canada Cataloguing in Publication

Choyce, Lesley, 1951–, author
The thing you're good at / Lesley Choyce.
(Orca soundings)

Issued in print and electronic formats.
ISBN 978-1-4598-1804-0 (softcover).—ISBN 978-1-4598-1805-7 (PDF).—
ISBN 978-1-4598-1806-4 (EPUB)

I. Title. II. Title: Thing you are good at. III. Series: Orca soundings
PS8555.H668T46 2018   jc813'.54   C2017-907682-5
C2017-907683-3

First published in the United States, 2018
Library of Congress Control Number: 2018933733

Summary: : In this high-interest novel for teen readers,
Jake tries to help his friend Maria after her parents are deported.
A free teacher guide for this title is available at orcabook.com.

MIX
Paper from
responsible sources
FSC® C016245

*Orca Book Publishers is dedicated to preserving the environment and has
printed this book on Forest Stewardship Council® certified paper.*

Orca Book Publishers gratefully acknowledges the support for its
publishing programs provided by the following agencies: the Government
of Canada through the Canada Book Fund and the Canada Council
for the Arts, and the Province of British Columbia through
the BC Arts Council and the Book Publishing Tax Credit.

Edited by Tanya Trafford
Cover images by Unsplash.com/Frank Mckenna (front) and
Shutterstock.com/Krasovski Dmitri (back)

ORCA BOOK PUBLISHERS
orcabook.com

Printed and bound in Canada.

21 20 19 18 • 4 3 2 1

ALSO BY LESLEY CHOYCE

Chapter One

My father didn't mean to be so nasty to me. It wasn't his fault.

He would sometimes (often, well, almost always) have a bad day at the fish-and-chip place he worked at called the Fish Shack. Only he called it the Shit Shack. He'd worked there ever since I could remember. And hated every minute of it. But he was always afraid to quit.

So when he had a *really* bad day, when customers sent back their fish, when the boss chomped on him a little too hard, he didn't have to tell me. I knew. He'd bring home a six-pack of malt liquor, and between that and the look on his face, I knew the story of the day. I could even predict the future. Me getting cursed at, shouted at, told outright I was a worthless little piece of shit. That sort of thing.

But nothing physical. He wasn't like that.

I always made sure my little brother, Luke, was out of the way though. I called him my little brother because he was a year younger than me, but he was actually quite a bit bigger than me. He was fifteen and walked around most of the time looking like someone had just told him some bad news. That might have been because there had been a lot of bad news in our lives.

I kept thinking that someday our luck was going to change.

Luke loved to watch old martial-arts movies with a headset on. And he studied books and instruction videos he'd signed out of the library, closing the door to our bedroom to practice whenever he could. He wanted to be a professional wrestler or mixed martial arts fighter when he grew up, even though I didn't think he had an aggressive bone in his body. I'd never seen him in a fight. He'd been picked on plenty, but I'd never seen him stand up for himself.

Like I said, we were a family that had had a lot of bad luck.

"Our luck ain't gonna change, Jake," my father always said. "Nothing is gonna change. No way, no how."

That was after malt-liquor bottle number one. I'd just nod and try to keep my mouth shut. I used to try

3

to change the subject. But that hardly ever worked.

"I'm sick and tired of smelling like fried fish," he would say. "No woman wants to be with a man who smells like old deep-fried seafood all the time."

I understood he missed the company of a woman. There was my mother once. A long while back. But she left after Luke was born. She claimed that living with us was a dead end. "I'm gonna find myself some opportunity," she said. And left. At least, that's what I remember. There was probably more to it than that.

My older brother, Cole, was in jail and had a couple more years to go. Everyone had expected him to get busted for selling drugs. But that isn't what happened. He was involved in a robbery of a gas station. How stupid is that? I was so angry at my brother for doing that. And I stayed angry at him.

I refused to talk to him when my father called him up on the phone each month.

As my dad got a little more drunk, he would remind me of my destiny: "None of you boys are gonna turn out to be any better off than me. If there's one thing I know, it's that."

It was always the same. Sometimes the words came out a little different, but after he said something along those lines, my dad would grit his teeth and then look like he was about to hit me. Funny—he never did though.

I tried not to take it personally. I figured he had to unload on someone. I was usually the one nearby.

Afterward he would shake his head and look like he was going to cry. But he never did that either.

"I'm sorry, Jake," he said each time. "I truly am. Will you forgive me?"

"Yes," I said.

I always said yes.

Chapter Two

We never ate fish at home. I guess you can figure out why. In the old days, my father would bring home leftover fish they were going to throw out, but now he was sick and tired of being around fish all day, so he didn't do that anymore.

In fact, I did a lot of the cooking. Spaghetti. Macaroni and cheese. Boiled potatoes. Cabbage, sometimes, but we had to open the windows because it made us all fart so much. I always meant to learn more about cooking and food but never seemed to get around to it.

But enough about food and farts.

I had two good friends in my miserable life. There was a girl named Maria. I met her when I was twelve. I was just standing there on the street, minding my own business, when she rode by on her bike. I smiled and said hi. She didn't hear me. But a few seconds later this car was coming down the road, and the driver was on his cell phone and didn't see her. He ran her off the road, and she fell onto the sidewalk. The guy driving just kept on going. I could see he was still on his damn phone.

I ran over to her and helped her up. She wasn't hurt bad. But her bike was wrecked. She didn't cry and, strangely, she didn't even seem angry. I started cursing that damn driver, but she just gave me a sad look. I apologized for cursing. I wanted to say something to make her feel better. But I didn't know what to say. So I walked her and her wrecked bike home. And that's how we became friends. Just like that.

We started hanging out together from then on. Neither one of us ever fit in anywhere at school. We both came from families that were dirt poor. Not that this was anything unusual in our part of the city. A lot of people were poor. I guess there were other reasons we didn't fit in. Other kids had labels for us. You know how school is. Everybody has a label. It's like it's stuck to your forehead or something.

You'd think school would be all about who is smart and who is stupid. But it isn't.

As far as I can tell, it's all about what you look like, who your parents are, what you wear and who you hang out with.

So Maria and I didn't hang out with anyone but ourselves. Sometimes Luke would tag along, but he usually didn't say a damn thing. Actually, when it was just Maria and me, we didn't even talk that much. But we were okay with that.

Maria had a mother and father, but neither seemed to stay at a job for more than a couple of weeks. I didn't know what that was about. But it sounded like they always had really crappy jobs, even worse than my dad's gig at the Fish Shack. Maria was an only child and said her mother couldn't have any more kids. And as it turned out, even though Maria and I had been friends for a long time, there was plenty about her life that I didn't know about.

Chapter Three

Sometimes I wondered why I never had many friends. When I asked my father about that, he explained it this way. *That's the kind of people we are. Anybody takes a look at any one of us and says to themselves, "I don't want to be seen with the likes of that."*

My dad usually cut my hair. Badly, with a pair of old scissors. He'd been doing that ever since we were little, and we all looked like we'd spent a month in prison. Maybe that's why my brother Cole ended up there. He already had the look.

One day I told my dad that I wanted to let my hair grow long. He said no at first, but I kept telling him this was something I really wanted to do. He finally shook his head. "Hell, son. Why not? You wanna be a hippie, go for it."

I said, "I don't wanna be a hippie. I just wanna see what I look like."

He laughed again. "All right. Go be Bob Marley, if you want, for all I care."

So my hair had a chance to start growing. I didn't look at all like Bob Marley, but I think it was around then that things started to change. I was still me. Looking mostly lost, walking around in my sad-looking old second-hand clothes that were ten years out of date.

We didn't have any shampoo around the house, so I had to use dish detergent, the cheap stuff. It always made my head kind of itchy, but, like a lot of things at home, I got used to it.

And like I said, I think something changed when my hair started to grow. No miracle or anything like that. But something.

A kid like me had two choices of what to do once the afternoon school bell rang and that part of the day was over. He could either go home, or he could hang out on the street. Some kids went to coffee shops or took buses to the malls on the other side of the city. But I never had any money to speak of. So all I had was the street.

And the big trouble with the street was that you ran into all kinds out there. Some of the other kids were doing the same thing I was, just trying to keep their heads down, stay under the radar of the nasty ones and just be. Most of the kids from my school who hung out on the street, well, most people would think they were downright criminals. But they weren't. Not all of them anyway.

They were wannabe criminals. Fakers. Like me, a lot of the others had watched their older brothers do real crimes, looking so cool doing what they were doing and then bragging about it. And they did seem cool to everybody, including me. Until they got taken off to jail like my brother Cole.

Leonard and Tom were a couple of the wannabes. They used to give me shit on the playground even when we were ten years old. When they got older, they started telling everyone to call them Leo and Toe. Everyone did. And for some reason, they decided to give me a break most days and not bust my chops.

Jake the Rake, they called me. Leo liked to say I wasn't worth his time.

"What's to pick on? Scrawny little thing, not much to him. He sits sideways in the classroom and the teacher can't see him so he gets marked absent."

I wasn't that skinny really. But when they noticed me changing my look, my hair getting longer, Toe said, "This is interesting. Jakey Rakey must be getting into drugs. I bet he's got his own stash of weed and has a marijuana plant growing in his closet."

Nope. No weed in my pocket. No plants in my closet. Not me. No way. No how.

On TV shows, parents always ask their kids, "How was school today?" But my father never did. He never asked much about anything I was up to. But Oscar asked me that question all the time. Oscar was friend number two.

Wednesday was trash day in my part of the city, so early on Wednesdays you'd see a few men and women out picking through trash bins in the neighborhood, looking for bottles and cans to recycle. That's how I met Oscar. He had an old shopping cart, and he always wore a suit and tie. The clothes looked like they'd never been washed and like he slept in them. This was because they probably never had been washed, and he *did* sleep in them. But the suit-and-tie thing was important to him.

I usually didn't have much to do after school and mostly wanted to avoid people like Toe and Leo, so Oscar would let me tag along while he did his "rounds."

Ours wasn't the best part of town for picking trash. I mean, there was plenty of trash but not a lot of recycling. Bottles and cans worth some money. So Oscar had his work cut out for him.

If you knew my part of the city, you'd know it wasn't anyplace you would want to live. There weren't a lot of jobs, so a lot of people were out of work. What work there was, well, mostly it was just crap jobs like the one my father had. And we all pretty much lived in crappy apartments, although some people were worse off and were, like Oscar, living on the street in cardboard boxes.

If you could, you moved out of this part of town. If you were a kid, you were stuck here until you graduated high school. Or until you quit. And if you quit, you usually ended up stuck here anyway. I didn't know why it worked that way. Maybe because there was no place else that wanted you.

Once upon a time…You know that phrase? They say that once upon a time, people had good jobs here. Or so my father says. But that was before my time.

Before the factories shut down, before the school went downhill, before the drugs and the gangs. That probably wasn't worth thinking about though. Now it just was what it was.

But Oscar never seemed to see it that way. He always tried to be optimistic. "I bet something good is just around the corner," he would say.

Chapter Four

A couple of weeks after I'd started to let my hair grow, I headed south on Duskie Street after school one day to look for Oscar. I liked hanging out with him because he saw the world so differently from everyone else.

I spotted him with his shopping cart from a ways off and waved. When he saw me he did his funny little bow.

I'd known Oscar for over a year, and he had never once seemed unhappy with where he was in life.

He was gently untying a blue bag when I caught up to him. Oscar picked trash like he was picking flowers in a field. "Whatever it is you do in life, Jacob, you gotta do it with respect," he said. He retrieved a Pepsi can and a wine bottle from the bag and then retied it with the utmost care. He held the wine bottle up to the light. "Western Cape, South Africa. Imagine that," he said. "This little bottle has probably seen more of the world than you or I ever will."

"And now it's going to end up at Dirty Dave's," I added. Dave's Recycling was where Oscar and most of the other shopping-cart people took their bottles and cans. Dave's was the only recycling depot in our part of town. They called the owner Dirty Dave not only because the place was so dirty but also because he regularly cheated homeless guys like Oscar out of a full refund.

The city didn't like anyone picking through the trash. They tried to crack down on scroungers and even fined them when they could. Dirty Dave knew no one cared about these people, so he only gave them 3.5 cents a can instead of the full 5 cents. For a wine bottle like the one he'd just found, Oscar would only get 7 cents instead of the usual 10. And no one could do a damn thing about it.

Oscar was still studying the light shining through the yellowish glass. "Once upon a time," he said wistfully, "I ordered a glass of wine in a fine restaurant. In fact, I did that more than once."

Oscar placed the bottle ever so gently into his cart and moved on down the street. "How was your day, Jacob?" he asked. He always called me Jacob, even though my real name is actually Jake. Oscar liked to be formal about things.

"Like every other day," I said.

"I don't believe that for a minute, Jacob," Oscar said, shaking his head. "Every day is different. Always something new. You just have to watch for it."

"I've been watching, just like you said. But they all seem pretty much the same to me."

Oscar laughed. "That's just 'cause you're so young. When you get older you'll have perspective."

"Right. So you want me to scout for you today?"

Oscar's broad smile always cheered me up. "Absolutely, my man. Last time you did that for me, my earnings increased by 45 percent."

I wasn't sure how he'd calculated that, but I was happy to help out. Scouting meant that I'd head off in some direction, looking for good trash.

Usually I walked, but today I felt like running. I'm not much of a runner, but sometimes it feels good. "I'll catch up with you in twenty minutes," I said, trotting off toward Jenkins Street. I had a hunch there'd be more bottles and cans there.

I ran past a couple of guys sitting on the front steps of an apartment building. "What you running for?" one of them asked me.

"Just running," I said, as politely as I could.

"Damn," the guy said. "No one is just running." I just kept going.

I found what I was hoping for in some big bins behind an old brick apartment building. The dumpster wasn't locked like a lot of them were these days. Inside was the mother lode.

I ran back and found Oscar still on Duskie. I was pretty excited to tell him what I'd found.

"Let's head on over there then," he said. "Jacob, you are nothing but good luck for me."

Once we got back to the dumpster, I climbed up into it and started tossing cans and bottles out to Oscar, who caught them with great flair. Before long his cart was overflowing. We'd scored at least a dozen wine bottles. Suddenly the back door of the apartment building opened, and someone started yelling at us.

"Get out of here, you two! Get the hell out, or I'm calling the cops."

I scrambled out of the dumpster. The guy from the apartment building picked up a rock and threw it at us. It clanged loudly against the trash bin.

Oscar nodded to the guy and told me to stay behind him as we rolled the full cart back toward the street. Oscar didn't seem particularly worried. But then, he wasn't much of a worrier. As we headed off to the depot he said, "You see, Jacob, what you had back there was a man who missed an opportunity."

"I don't get it," I said.

"Well, what he saw was a couple of trash pickers, and he decided we were up to no good. He lashed out like that because he couldn't see the truth of the situation. He missed a great opportunity too. He missed the chance to get to know two fine gentlemen with some insight into life's hard lessons."

"I'm not sure I ever considered myself a gentleman," I said. "And I don't think I have any insight into life's hard lessons."

"Well, that's where you'd be wrong, my friend. You have far more insight than you know."

Chapter Five

School. What kid really wants to talk about what happens at school? You go there, you put in your time. You try to keep your head down so you don't get noticed. You try to stay out of the way of people like Leo and Toe. You sit in the back of the room so you don't get called on in class as much. You get tired of the way some kids look at you. If you are lucky, you find someone in the cafeteria to eat your crappy baloney sandwich with.

That someone for me was Maria. Don't think Maria was, like, my girlfriend or anything. We were just comfortable with each other. Sometimes Maria didn't have any lunch, so I'd give her half of mine.

Maria had long dark hair that she'd let hang down in front of her face sometimes, like she was hiding behind it. She liked to wear a baggy, oversized hoodie, and she'd tuck her hands up into the sleeves. If anybody gave her a hard time about the way she looked, she didn't react visibly. It was like she pretended not to hear. But I knew the words hurt her. I think she actually had a powerful quiet spirit, and I admired that. I knew things were pretty tough for her at home, and school wasn't much better.

And then this funny thing happened at school. Mr. Clemson, our history teacher, had to take some time off because of something that happened in the principal's office. Though nobody knew for sure, rumors were going around that he'd freaked out and started yelling at Mrs. Warren, our principal. They called it stress leave, but who knows.

That wasn't the funny part. Funny as in good, by the way. Mr. Clemson was replaced by a new guy, Mr. Lotz. Jim Lotz. He was, like, just out of college or something, and the complete opposite of Clemson. Clemson was old. Lotz was young. Clemson, I think, hated all of us. Lotz seemed to like us. Clemson was tall and skinny, while Lotz was built like a football player—big and stocky.

Clemson had never told a joke. I never once saw him laugh. But Lotz told jokes all the time, even though they were lame. On his first day in our Modern History class, in the middle of introducing himself, he paused and said, "I'm reading a book about antigravity. It's impossible to put down."

We didn't get it. No one laughed. He tried again.

"I can't believe I got fired from the calendar factory," he said. "All I did was take a day off."

I smiled. So did Maria. The rest of the kids just stared at him like he was a lunatic. But he didn't give up.

"I wasn't originally going to get a brain transplant," Lotz continued, having a hard time keeping a straight face, "but then I changed my mind."

Some kids groaned. I laughed out loud. Man, I hadn't laughed in a long time.

Clemson never went off topic. He was all about the textbook. But Lotz loved to tell stories. Pretty soon kids figured out they could easily distract Lotz and get him to ramble about his life or talk about what he called his "personal philosophy." We started calling him Lotz of Stories. Or Lotz of Ideas. He admitted to us that this was his first teaching job. You could tell he hadn't grown up poor like many of us. Some kids referred to him as "shiny" because he was like something shiny and new that hadn't gotten dirty yet or worn out. On that first day he declared he hated the textbook we were using, that it was only one version of history and that this version sucked. Yeah, he used that word. Then he threw it in the trash can.

That really got our attention.

Lotz was a younger version of Oscar in a way. A young Oscar with a college education, better clothes and no shopping cart.

Kids gave Mr. Lotz a hard time at first, partly because he was shiny and new and partly because they didn't know what to do with a teacher like him, who seemed way too happy to be here teaching us.

Right after the trash-can incident, Toe stood up and said, "Who da fuck do you think you are? You think you know more about history than what's in that book?" This, as you can imagine, seemed like a really weird thing for Toe to do, but Toe's special passion in life was giving teachers a hard time. That is, when he wasn't harassing other students. But Lotz had thrown Toe off his game, I think.

Mr. Lotz just smiled. "Well, maybe," he said. "Maybe not. That's not for me to say. That's for you to judge. And you're right to challenge me. That's good. I like to be challenged. That's what's going to make this class interesting. Anyone else care to add to this discussion?"

But no one raised their hands. No one quite knew how to cope with a teacher who didn't yell at you or send you to Mrs. Warren's office for disrupting the class.

And so school started to seem a little different. My hair kept getting longer, and now I had Mr. Lotz's class to look forward to. As the days went by it seemed like there was more and more personal philosophy and less and less modern history.

"Jake," Mr. Lotz said after class one day, "I've been watching you. You don't talk much, do you?"

I shook my head.

"But I can see that you're listening," he said. "And, more important, I can see that you're thinking. What do you think about?"

"I dunno," I said. "I guess I just think about some of the things you've been saying."

"Very cool," he said, nodding. "Very cool indeed. So, Jake. Have you ever heard of the term *self-actualization*?"

Only someone as shiny and fresh out of college as him would have used a word like that in a conversation with the likes of me.

"Self what?"

"Self-actualization. It's a word used to describe the process of reaching your full potential."

"Sounds like a lot of work."

"So you've never heard either of your parents use that word?"

I almost broke out laughing. I imagined my father coming home from work one evening and saying, "Down at the Shit Shack, me and some of the kitchen staff were thinking we needed a bit more self-actualization around here."

"Hello, Jake. Are you still there?"

"Sorry. Answer is no. My father has never used that word, and my mother, well, she's long gone."

"Oh. Sorry."

"No worries."

Mr. Lotz wrote the word down on a yellow sticky note and handed it to me. "Here, this is for you. I want you to look it up next time you're at a computer. And keep it on you. Words have power. This is your word."

Just then kids for the next class started streaming in, and that was the end of that.

Chapter Six

I walked Maria home that afternoon. It was the first time I'd done that in a long while. It wasn't that she didn't like being with me. I just think she didn't want anyone, even me, to see where she lived.

I was telling her about the conversation I'd had with Mr. Lotz when she started to cry.

I think I'd seen Maria cry only one time before, and it was years ago. I never knew what she was crying about back then, and when I asked she just ran away from me.

This time was different.

"Wanna talk about it?" I asked.

"Not really," she answered. Which I totally understood. Whenever anyone asked me to talk about my problems or myself, I said the same thing. But Maria kept crying.

So I did something I had never done before. I put my arm around her. I almost expected her to push me away. But she didn't. She leaned into me and sobbed. I could feel her body shaking, and her tears soaked my shirt. I never even knew someone could cry that much.

We were in the middle of the sidewalk in front of her ragged-ass apartment building. People had to walk around us, and they were giving me dirty looks, like I was the one who had made this girl cry. People had been giving me dirty looks most of my life, so I was used to it. So we just stood there.

When she finally stopped crying, she said, "I'm sorry."

"Nothing to be sorry about," I said.

She nodded toward the front door of her building. "I don't want to go in."

"Why?"

"No one will be there. Just me. And I hate this place."

"I'll go in with you," I said.

"I'd rather you didn't."

"Why not?"

She didn't have an answer. She shrugged, took a deep breath and led me into her building.

The front door wasn't locked, and the hallway was littered with old chip bags, cans and bottles and some stacked-up cardboard boxes. The stairs creaked as we walked up to the third floor. The hallway wasn't much better, and I could see rat poop along the baseboard.

Maria opened a door without using a key. "The lock's broke," she said. "My dad says there's no point in fixing it. We won't be here very long."

I just nodded. There were more cardboard boxes inside, stacked against the walls.

"And there's not much worth stealing, I guess," she added.

I sat down on a ripped-up vinyl sofa that looked like something you'd see left by the side of the road. Maria looked embarrassed.

My wet shirt was giving me the chills. As I tried to pull it away from my skin, Maria said, "Sorry about that. I don't usually cry. Well, not in front of anyone."

"You can cry in front of me any time you want," I said. Silly thing to say.

"I'll remember that," Maria said. "I'll get you a towel. You want something to drink? Coke or something?"

"Sure."

Maria walked into the tiny kitchen and opened the most beat-up refrigerator I'd seen in my life. She took out a big plastic bottle of cola and poured me a glass.

I smiled and took a sip. It was cold and flat. "Um. Good. Thanks," I said.

Maria wasn't drinking anything. She sat down beside me on the vinyl couch and became real quiet. She cleared her throat. "Jake, I have something I have to tell you."

I tried to take another sip of the flat cola, but it was like my throat muscles wouldn't work. This something-I-have-to-tell-you thing sounded important and, to be truthful, kind of scary. Although my throat wasn't working, my brain was in overdrive.

Holy crap, what was she about to say? Was she gonna say she was in love with me? Was she going to say she was pregnant by some guy? Was she going to tell me she was suicidal? I was afraid to hear what would come next. It could be something good or bad, really good or really bad, and whatever it was I wasn't sure I wanted to hear it.

"Jake, see those boxes?"

"Uh-huh."

"We haven't even unpacked. Like I said, I think we are going to have to move again. And I don't think it will be anywhere nearby. I may never see you again."

My brain kind of went numb right then. Maria was a big part of what little bit of good I had going.

I set the glass down on the table in front of me. "I don't want you to go," I said. And then I added something stupid. "Who would I hang out with at school?"

Maria looked down at the glass on the table. "You'd find someone else," she said. "I know you'll be okay."

"Why do you have to move?" I asked.

"My parents...you know how they're always changing jobs? It's because they always have to work off the record. You know, under the table."

"How come?"

"Because they're in the country illegally."

"What's the big deal?" I asked. "I thought there were lots of people like that."

"Yeah, there are. But things are changing. The government's starting to crack down. My parents could get arrested and deported."

"Deported? Like, kicked out of the country?"

"Yeah. That's why we keep moving. But lately we've heard of others being arrested and being held in detention centers. It's getting pretty bad. So my parents are thinking of leaving the country before things get worse."

"But what about you? Why do you have to go?"

Maria looked at me in surprise. "They're my parents, that's why."

"Oh." I was only thinking about me, not Maria and her family's problem. I was thinking I was about to lose one of my only friends.

"There must be something they can do," I said. "Can't they talk to someone and straighten things out? Fill out some papers or something? Get one of those free lawyers?"

"They think if they go to the government for anything, they'll be in trouble. They're scared now. We've seen it happen to others, some of the people they were working with."

This wasn't right. There had to be a way. Maria and her parents had as much right to live here as I did.

"Hey, weren't you born here?" I asked.

"Yes. I was born right here in the city."

"Then you *do* have a right to stay. You can't kick out a kid who was born here and has lived her whole life here. In a couple of years you'll graduate and get a job and be like everybody else. Nobody can make you leave."

"I don't think it's that simple. But anyway, I have to go where my parents go."

"Do you *want* to leave?"

"Of course not."

"Then I'll help you figure something out," I said, sounding like I knew what the hell I was talking about. But I was just bluffing.

She touched the spot on my shirt where her tears had dried and said nothing at all.

Chapter Seven

Maria's parents arrived home about ten minutes later, and they didn't seem at all happy to see me in the house. Her mother seemed a little frightened, and her father looked me up and down like I'd just said something really nasty.

"You remember Jake," Maria said.

Both parents tried to smile, but they didn't quite succeed.

"I better go," I said. "Bye, Maria." And I left.

I didn't feel like going home after that. I knew Oscar was in another part of town, collecting his bottles and cans. I didn't know where else to go, so I decided to just hang out at the library on Fourteenth Street. I sat down at one of the public computers. I hardly even knew how to use it. Guess what? There'd never been a computer in my house. Not even video games. We had an old TV, that's all. And three channels.

I watched the other kids on computers. Some were playing games, some were looking at different websites. I stared at the Google page and didn't even know where to begin. I pulled out the piece of paper Mr. Lotz had given me. I typed in the letters.

Self-actualization, I read. *Achieving a person's full potential and becoming a complete person; to understand oneself as an independent, creative, fulfilled person.*

I almost laughed out loud. I didn't think I really even understood the words. To me, it sounded totally like one of those bullshit things I'd read somewhere before, the kind of thing that would apply to some happy person somewhere on the planet but not to anyone in my neighborhood.

I clicked on the word *Images* and saw photos of athletic-looking people standing on beaches or on mountain-tops with their arms outstretched. The sun was shining, and it made me think they all must live in some fantasy world somewhere or just in someone's imagi-nation. There were images of pyramids too, and I didn't get that.

None of it had any real meaning to me. I typed in another word. *Deportation.*

That took me to some news articles and speeches by politicians. None of what I read helped. The news was all bad. People who were in the country illegally could be deported at any time. The government was stepping up its program in a lot of cities, including mine.

I left the library feeling pretty hopeless. Lotz and his stupid word. Stupid laws that didn't allow people to live where they wanted to live. There should be a law, I kept thinking, some law that says if you only have two real friends in the world, no one should be allowed to take one of them away.

The next day I sat with Maria at the back of Mr. Lotz's class. I didn't want to tell her about what I'd read in the library or say anything about her leaving in case she started crying. Instead, I wrote her a note saying I

would always, always be her friend.
I passed it to her just before the bell
rang. She read it and smiled.

As soon as class started, Lotz of
Stories started talking to us like he
was bursting. Like he'd had one too
many Red Bulls. He got going about
Gandhi and Martin Luther King and
Nelson Mandela. And most of it went
right over our heads. But the guy had
so much enthusiasm. I think we all sat
there a little stunned, even Leo and Toe.
Lotz didn't run out of steam until the
bell rang again and kids started to pour
out of his classroom. I heard Leo say on
the way out, close enough to Lotz that
he would hear, "Man, I'm glad that's
over. I thought he was gonna have a
heart attack or something."

I was one of the last to leave, and Lotz
tugged my sleeve and pulled me back.

"So did you look it up?"

I didn't want to tell him I thought it was a crock of shit, so I said no.

Lotz looked disappointed. "Okay, but carry it with you, okay? You never know what could happen."

I said okay, even though I had thrown the sticky note into the trash at the library. I started to walk away, but he tugged at my sleeve again. That kind of seemed weird for a teacher to do. If he'd done that to Leo, I knew Leo would have punched him right in the face.

"Here's the thing," Mr. Lotz said. "I'm new at this school, and I know I don't know much about your life or the lives of your classmates."

I wanted to say, *That's right. You don't know a damn thing about us, and all your fancy ideas are wasted on us.* But I didn't.

Lotz continued. "See, I have this theory. I think anyone, *anyone*, can be a success if they can find one solid thing they are good at. They just need to find that one thing and make it work for them. That's what you need to do, Jake. Find that thing and make it work for you."

His words, like those words on the computer screen in the library, were just that—words. Ideas. Nothing to do with real life.

"Why not give it a try, Jake? Figure out what it is you're good at," Mr. Lotz said with a big smile, "and really work at it."

I had to say something, I guessed. But this shiny guy, this long-winded, overly educated teacher, was living in some imaginary world that had nothing to do with me. So I told him the truth.

"Yeah, the only problem is, Mr. Lotz, I'm not good at nothing."

He looked puzzled at first, deflated. But then he put his smile back on.

"Anything," he said. "You're supposed to say, 'I'm not good at anything.'" And then Mr. Lotz looked me straight in the eye and said, "Just think about it, Jake. Think about what I said."

Chapter Eight

I felt bad that I had given Lotz a hard time. He seemed to have taken a real interest in me, which was both good and bad. I preferred to go unnoticed. But his words stayed with me. *Not good at nothing. Not good at anything.* What was the difference? I tried to think about people I knew. What were they good at, and how did they use it?

My dad was good at complaining. And that hadn't gotten him anywhere.

My brother Cole was good at getting into trouble. And that got him in jail.

My brother Luke was good at keeping to himself. And I didn't see that doing him much good.

My mother had been good at running away from our sorry life. Maybe that *did* work for her.

Leo and Toe were good at giving people a hard time. That didn't sound like much of a career either, but they were always pretty proud of themselves.

And Maria? Even though I'd known her for years, she was still a bit of a mystery. I didn't know what she was good at. She never liked to talk much about herself.

Maybe Oscar was a better example. He was good at putting a positive spin on anything and making the best of what he had. But he was still homeless and living on the street. Although sometimes he stayed at the men's shelter downtown.

And me? I really didn't know what I was good at. Nobody had ever said to me, *Jakey, you're really good at…* whatever.

Maria was waiting for me outside the school when classes ended. She looked so sad. I kept thinking about what she had told me and wondered if she would really have to move away.

"Hey," I said.

"Hey, Jake. How was your day?"

"Like all the rest," I answered, but then I thought about what Oscar had said about each day being an adventure or something. So I told her about my chat with Mr. Lotz after history class.

"Why do you think he said that to you and not the whole class?" she asked as we walked down the sidewalk.

"I don't know."

"I think I know what you're good at," she said with a hint of a smile.

"What?"

"You're good at..." She paused and looked up at the sky. "You're good at helping people."

"Bullshit," I said. "Who have I ever really helped?"

"Me, for one. You're always there for me when I'm feeling down."

"That's not a skill."

"Well, I think it is. And there's Oscar. You like helping him out, right? And Luke. You're always looking out for Luke."

"That's nothing. He's my brother."

"But I've watched you, Jake. You do things for people sometimes, and you don't expect anything in return. Not a lot of people are like that. Most people I know only do something good for a person if they expect to be paid for it or get something for themselves.

But not you. So there. You're good at something."

"I don't know if that's true. But thanks for saying it. You make me sound like a saint. Believe me, I'm no saint."

"I should call you Saint Jake."

"Saint Loser is more like it."

Maria gave me a soft punch on the shoulder. Right then I noticed a pickup truck coming up alongside us. The brakes squealed as the truck came to a stop. I could hear a loud, nasty rap song playing inside. Maria looked a little scared as the driver rolled down the window.

"Jakey," the driver said. It was Dalton, one of Cole's friends from back before he got sent off to prison. Dalton had been looking for trouble as much as Cole was, and I usually hadn't wanted to know what the two of them had done together. But Dalton had always been okay to me.

"Hey, Dalton," I said. "Where'd you get the truck?"

"I stole it, little man," he said, turning down his car stereo.

"Lookin' to join Cole?" I asked.

Dalton just laughed. He turned off the engine and leaned out the window. "I'm just messin' with you, Jake. I don't do any of that shit anymore. I bought this here truck, fair and square. Four months with the paving company. Worst four months of my life. But it got me this. You guys want a ride?"

I looked at Maria, who still seemed a little scared, but I told her it would be okay. I couldn't even remember the last time I'd been in a ride other than a bus. "Sure," I said. I knew I could trust Dalton. "A ride would be great."

I walked Maria around to the passenger's side, and we got in. The inside was a bit smelly. Old cigarette smoke and a guy who hadn't had a bath in a while.

But it was warm, and Dalton seemed really happy to have some company.

"You guys hungry?" he asked.

I'd shared my peanut-butter-and-jelly sandwich at lunch with Maria. I was hungry most days, and I knew Maria was hungrier than me. "I don't have any money," I said.

"It's on me," Dalton said. "I still got some of that paving money left. My treat."

"Why are you doing this?" I asked.

"I don't know. I still feel bad about Cole, I guess. It easily could have been me. How's he doing?"

"Okay, I guess. We don't really hear from him much." I didn't give Dalton the truth. That I was still angry at Cole and refused to talk to him on the phone or visit him.

"Your brother getting busted was an eye-opener for me," Dalton said. "Like a big slap of icy cold water in the face.

I decided to cut myself free from all the bad stuff I could. It wasn't easy, man. Took me a while to figure out what to do. I worked some easy-ass jobs but didn't make much dough. Then I got on the paving crew. But just long enough to buy this. Now I'm using it to do odd jobs, haul stuff for people."

"How's it working out?"

"Well, not that good so far. I don't know how to get the word out. And everyone I know is too poor to want to pay me to haul anything. But I'll get there."

We pull up in front of McDonald's. "Mickey D's," Dalton said. "Hope you guys ain't vegetarians."

Chapter Nine

Dalton had dropped out of high school a couple of years back. *I just got tired of showing up every morning*, is the way he explained it at the time. This didn't really make sense to me at the time, because he didn't really have anything else to do that I could see. As a lot of other kids like him did, he'd just hang out on the street until he found a way to get into trouble or until trouble found him.

Cole had actually stayed in school. In fact, he'd kept giving me lectures about sticking with school and graduating. He'd even helped me with my math homework. I'd always thought of him as smarter than me. But then, robbing a store isn't most people's idea of smart.

The hamburger Dalton bought for me tasted good, even though I knew it wasn't exactly healthy. But then, when you don't have much money and eat the same thing all the time, even a Big Mac tastes good. I watched Maria eat hers very slowly as Dalton rambled on.

"That truck out there is the thing that's gonna save my sorry ass," he said. "Sure, it needs some work. But now when things at home get a little too heavy, I can just grab my keys and go sleep in my truck."

Dalton's father was a mean drunk. When my father drank, he sometimes got mad, and if I was the only one around he sometimes said mean things to me, raising his voice until he was screaming. But then he would stop, and usually he'd tell me he was sorry. Dalton's father wasn't like that. Once he got drinking, it got ugly. And he liked to hit. Hard. So I could see why Dalton was happy about the idea of sleeping in his truck.

When Dalton finished eating, he tapped his fingers on the table. "Gotta go," he said, even though I doubted he had anywhere to go to. "You guys want me to take you home?"

I looked at Maria. I could tell she liked being here. And besides, we weren't far from home.

"No thanks, Dalton," I said. "Hey, man, thanks for this. Nobody's been this nice to me for a long while."

"No problem, little brother. Just trying to spread the wealth."

After Dalton left, Maria and I just sat there in McDonald's, saying nothing and watching people coming in and going out. Families. Real families. Mothers with little kids. Fathers with sons. "It's just like you see on TV," I said to Maria finally. But then I remembered Maria didn't have a TV.

"I bet they have problems too," Maria said. "We all have problems."

"Yeah," I said. "Probably." But there wasn't much probably about it. Sure, they had problems, but not quite like mine. And not quite like Maria's.

I guess I had a hangdog look on my face, because she suddenly got a little devilish smile on hers, picked up a French fry and flipped it at me, hitting me in the nose.

"Hey!" I said, totally shocked by this totally un-Maria-like move.

"Hey," she repeated, stifling a laugh. "Can't we forget about our problems just for once?"

I nodded, smiled and flipped a fry back at her.

Eventually we got up and dumped our trays, and I walked her home. She asked me not to come in this time. On the way to my place I realized I had a bad feeling in my gut. I thought about Dalton, trying to figure out how to make a life for himself with that old truck. I thought about my own father, sticking with the crappy Fish Shack job he hated just to keep himself and his sons from ending up on the street.

And I thought about Maria and her parents. They weren't hurting a damn soul. Why should they be persecuted like this?

And then I thought about what Mr. Lotz had said to me. What was I good at?

The answer still seemed to be nothing. Maria was wrong. I couldn't do anything to help anybody around here. Not even myself.

Chapter Ten

I went back to the library because I couldn't think of any other place to go. I sat down and read some newspapers and then went on the library computer again to find out more about what was going on with this deportation of illegal immigrants. I guess this had already been going on in many parts of the country, but, like Maria said, now the authorities were cracking down on people right here in the city, right here in my neighborhood.

I thought it was downright cruel. I mean, when you think about people just disappearing, you think about zombies coming and stealing them or criminals kidnapping them or something like that. You don't think about cops or government agents just going into people's homes and taking them away, never to be seen again.

The more I read, the more it seemed that Maria's family had just been lucky so far. But luck always runs out.

I made a point of hanging out with Maria whenever I could. More than ever, I felt like it was my job to protect her, even though I wasn't sure who exactly I was protecting her from. Could some government guy just show up and grab her? That sounded too crazy. This wasn't like Nazi Germany or anything.

I also asked Luke to keep a watch out for her, although I didn't say why.

"Yeah," said Luke. "I'll make sure nobody messes with her."

And I knew Luke would do just that.

When a week went by and nothing happened, I started to believe that Maria and her parents were going to be okay. Maybe they were just being paranoid.

A second week went by and nothing bad happened. I kept checking the news at the library in school when I could. It seemed like the crackdown on illegals might have slowed. Or maybe it was just old news.

Dalton saw the two of us walking home again one day and stopped to give us a ride. He had a truckload of junk in the back. "I'm hauling it to the dump," he said, proud as could be. "My uncle asked me to clean out his basement.

If I can get more jobs like this, I'll be all set."

I couldn't see how owning an old beat-up truck could make a guy so happy, but it seemed to have changed Dalton, who had always seemed to me like a ship without a rudder.

It was like he was reading my mind, because the next thing he said was, "This ain't just no ordinary truck, ya know. This is a Ford F-150."

Maria and I both nodded like we were impressed.

On Friday I saw a black government car parked in front of the school. At least, I thought it was a government car. It looked like something you'd see in one of those spy movies. It got me worried, but nothing came of it. Maybe it was just a black car and that was all.

The next Wednesday, I asked Maria if she wanted to come help me do my rounds with Oscar. It was a fairly sunny day, and I thought it might help keep her mind off her worries.

We scouted cans and bottles and stuffed them into an old backpack I'd found.

"Things just keep getting better and better," Oscar said when I carried my first load back to him. I told him I thought there were some good finds a few blocks over, past Duskie.

We walked Oscar and his cart over there, and he found a whole case of empty wine bottles sitting at the curb. He inspected them one by one as he put them in his cart. "Australia, Italy, France, New Zealand," he said. "This is just like traveling around the world. I sure am glad you two bought me the ticket and are here to enjoy the trip."

Maria looked at me and just smiled. Today was a good day.

Chapter Eleven

And then it happened.

Monday rolled around, and Maria wasn't in school. I kept hoping she'd show up late, but she didn't. The usual kids were entering Mr. Lotz's class for third period, but she wasn't one of them. I stopped at Lotz's desk and just stood there for a minute, still hoping she'd arrive.

"What's up, Jake?" he asked.

"I'm worried about Maria."

"Why is that?"

"I can't say."

"Oh. Well, is there anything I can do to help?"

"I don't think so. But I want to go look for her. Can I skip class?"

He looked at me, and I could see the concern in his eyes. "Of course. Do what you have to do."

And I left.

I ran as long as I could toward her apartment building, but my lungs gave out on me after a few blocks. I was still winded when I got there and struggled a bit walking up the three flights of stairs.

The door was unlocked. I called out a hello as I walked in. But no one was there. I had a sick feeling in the pit of my stomach. Nothing looked much different about the place. Some dirty dishes in the sink, some papers on the table, but somehow it had the feel of a place that had been abandoned in a hurry.

That sick feeling didn't go away. I felt a kind of panic set in. Like my brain was freezing up. *She's gone now, and there is nothing you can do about it*, I told myself. *You should have taken better care of her.*

I sat down on a folding metal chair at the kitchen table. Then there was another voice. I swear it was Maria's. *Don't give up on me, Jake. Don't give up.* But the voice was just in my head.

I could feel my heart beating faster. I closed my eyes and tried to breathe through the panic. I couldn't believe she had moved away without telling me, without even saying goodbye. I guess I thought she'd always be there for me— someone I could be around without feeling like she wanted something from me, someone I could talk to, even though we didn't do much talking. And now this.

I opened my eyes and looked around. It didn't really look like anyone had packed up and left. I walked into Maria's room. All her stuff was still there. And in her parents' room I saw clothes in the closet and boxes of their things on the floor.

Something didn't seem right.

Chapter Twelve

I don't know why I thought about turning to Dalton. Dalton was pretty clueless about a lot of things, but then again, he had that truck. That Ford F-150. And he had been a close friend of Cole. Almost like family for a while, before Cole started getting deeper into trouble.

Dalton's parents lived in the same part of town as Maria, and as I approached his big ugly apartment complex, I saw his truck parked outside. There was newspaper taped up on the inside of his windows. I peeked in through a small space between sheets and saw him lying there on the seat.

I tapped gently on the window.

Nothing.

I tapped harder and said his name.

Dalton woke up, startled, then tore down one of the pieces of newspaper and saw it was me. He slowly opened the passenger door.

"Jakey, what're you doing 'round here?"

"It's Maria. She's missing."

"Missing? What do you mean?"

I climbed into the truck cab as Dalton slid over to the driver's seat. I explained what I thought had happened.

Dalton just shook his head. "I don't know nothing about any of that shit.

And it sounds like some pretty deep shit. I don't trust nothing about the government. I don't know what you think I can do."

I desperately wanted an ally. Dalton was older than me, but he was also just an out-of-school teenager who slept in his truck. Not exactly someone with a lot of brains and know-how.

"No way," he continued. "I don't want nothing to do with messing with the government."

I didn't know what he was picturing. The two of us storming into wherever they were with machine guns? But I got the picture. I opened the door to leave.

Dalton grabbed my wrist. "Wait. I'll drive you wherever you need to go. Just don't get me into any kind of trouble with the government or the cops."

"Okay."

"Okay, what? Where do you want to go?"

Where did I want to go? I didn't know anything about immigration laws, detention centers, illegal immigrants. Shit, where did I want to go?

"School," I said. "Take me to school."

The guard at the school entrance gave me a hard time about showing up in the middle of the day, but he let me in. I walked to Mr. Lotz's classroom and could see through the window of the door that he was in the middle of one of his long lectures about something or other. I took a deep breath and knocked.

Mr. Lotz put his hand up to the class, then came my way, opened the door and walked out into the hall. He saw the look on my face. "Jake, what's up?"

I tapped the door closed behind him. I told him about Maria and her family.

I told him I was pretty sure they'd been taken away by government people.

Lotz nodded his head up and down. "I've been reading about it in the papers. I had no idea there were so many kids at this school whose parents are living here illegally."

"Will you help me?"

Lotz suddenly looked puzzled. "Why me?"

I shrugged. I didn't really have an answer. "I guess I don't have anyone else I can turn to, anyone else I can trust."

Lotz ran a hand across his forehead and then stroked his chin. "Jesus, Jake. I don't know if there's anything I can do."

"Will you at least help me find out if Maria's family is being held at the detention center? I need to know."

Mr. Lotz didn't answer right away. "Yeah, I'll try to help," he said after a few moments. "Let me see if I can get someone to cover my class. But we'll have to call a cab. I don't have a car."

"I've got wheels," I said. "I just need you."

Mr. Lotz ducked back into his class, spoke to his students briefly and then hurried me to the office. I waited in the hall until he came out.

"Mrs. Warren was cool about it," he said. "And she gave me Maria's file. It has some info about her parents."

We started walking toward the guard at the exit. He looked at us kind of funny, but he didn't say a word as he opened the door for us and we walked out of the school.

Dalton gave me a dirty look when I opened the door to his truck. I'm guessing he didn't like the look of Mr. Lotz.

"Who's this?" he asked.

"Mr. Lotz. He's a teacher," I said.

Dalton didn't have to say what he was thinking. I'd heard him say it plenty of times when he was still in school. Dalton hated teachers. All of them.

Mr. Lotz thrust his hand toward Dalton. "Jim Lotz," he said. "Jake asked me to see what I could do. I couldn't say no."

Dalton reluctantly shook his hand and nodded his head for us to get in.

"Where to now?" Dalton asked.

Mr. Lotz was on his phone, looking something up. "Okay. Got it. Head downtown. Take Lombard Avenue, and then go east on Hastings."

"Whatever you say, Teach," Dalton said.

As we headed toward downtown, I noticed how carefully Dalton was driving. Not too fast, not too slow, looking in his mirrors when he changed lanes, staying right at the speed limit.

It made me think about what Lotz had said again. *One good thing.* Dalton had it. Not much but something. He was a good driver. And he had a truck. And he was there to help me. That was three good things, actually.

"What do we do when we get there?" I asked.

Lotz was still pecking away at his phone. He nodded and then pecked away some more and then said, "Okay" out loud.

"Okay, what?" I asked.

"Okay. I know where they hold illegal immigrants. And I know we need an immigration lawyer. But first we need to confirm that Maria's parents are being detained."

"How do we do that?" I wanted to know.

"We go in and ask." Then he corrected himself. "No. I go in and ask. They are obliged to tell me, but they probably won't let me speak to them without the lawyer."

Mr. Lotz saw the worried look on my face. "Sorry, Jake. One step at a time. Get the facts, assess the situation, come up with a plan."

I don't know what I was thinking. We'd maybe go there and magically the doors would open and Maria and her family could come home with us? "Sounds like something out of a textbook," I said a bit sarcastically.

"Probably is."

We sat in silence as Dalton carefully guided his truck through traffic, taking directions from Mr. Lotz, until we arrived at a tall, nearly windowless building in a part of the city I'd never even been to before.

Mr. Lotz gripped the file tightly as he got out of the truck. "Wish me luck," he said and walked toward the building. He was stopped at the door by a security guard, and after they'd had a brief conversation, we watched him go in.

Chapter Thirteen

We waited in the truck for over an hour.
I was getting real antsy.

"Be cool," Dalton said. "Sometimes
all you can do is wait."

So we waited some more.

Finally Mr. Lotz emerged from the
building. When he got into the truck,
he looked at me and said, "She's not
there."

I didn't know whether to be happy or worried.

"But her parents are," he continued. "The guy I talked to looked them up on the computer, and he confirmed that they have been detained and are going to be deported soon. But I wasn't allowed to talk to them."

"So Maria must be hiding somewhere. We have to find her."

"Where do we start?" Dalton asked. "I'll take you anywhere you need to go. This is getting interesting."

But it didn't get interesting. It just got frustrating. We went back to Maria's apartment. We looked in every room and every closet. No sign of her. We drove up and down the streets, and then, as it started to get dark, we dropped Mr. Lotz off at the school.

"I'm going to make a few calls to see if I can find someone to help out with Maria's parents," he said before closing the truck door. "Maybe we should ask for help to find Maria."

"No," I said. "We can't ask the police. We can't do that. She'd end up like her parents, and I'd never see her again."

Lotz looked worried. He wrote something on a slip of paper and handed it to me. "This is my cell phone. Call if you think I can do anything."

Dalton dropped me off at my apartment building. I felt lost and defeated. "Don't give up hope, little man," he said. "She's hiding somewhere—you know it. She's free, and that's a start."

As I walked up the stairs to my apartment, I thought about Maria out there somewhere, all on her own and scared as hell. I went in and sat down at the kitchen table, realizing I'd probably just lost the one really good thing in my life. I had that familiar nasty feeling in the pit of my stomach. I realized I might never see Maria again. We were much more than just friends. I still didn't think of her as a girlfriend, not like the way other guys talked about their girlfriends. But she'd been there for me when I felt really down. She was my ally in a hostile world. Now I didn't have any allies—not like her anyway.

There was a knock on the door. I got up and opened it.

It was Maria. She looked scared. Really scared.

I let her inside immediately. I looked up and down the hall. No one was there. No one was looking. "You okay?"

"They took my parents," she said. "Three men, they just showed up and took them away."

"Where were you?"

"My mother told me to go in my bedroom before they opened the door. But when I heard them arguing, I got scared and went out on the fire escape.

I stayed there until they were gone. I knew what was happening. I just froze. I couldn't move. Now I wish I had gone with my parents. I want to be with them."

"Don't say that. You're here now. You're safe."

Maria shook her head. "Will you take me to where they are being held? I need to be with them. I don't care what it's like there. If they are going to be deported, I want to go with them. They're my parents."

I understood what she was feeling, but I didn't want to lose her. Sure, she wanted to be with her parents. But then I'd never see her again.

"I know what you're saying, but you're here now. You're safe. You can stay here with me until we figure something out."

I made Maria a peanut-butter-and-jelly sandwich. There wasn't much else in the house. But she didn't eat it. I looked at the clock on the stove and realized my father would be home any minute.

Minutes later I heard him in the hall, fumbling with his keys and cursing. It was his usual mood when he came home from work.

When the door opened and he walked in with a couple of bags of groceries, he looked first at Maria and then at me. He'd met Maria a number of times, but he'd hardly ever said anything to her. Maybe he didn't like her because she wasn't like us, or maybe he didn't like me having a girl for a friend. I never knew.

"Looks like we got company," he said flatly.

"Maria needs our help," I said.

"She in some kind of trouble? 'Cause we got enough trouble of our own. We don't need to take on someone else's grief."

"They took her parents," I said.

"They who?"

"The immigration people. They're in the detention center and are going to be kicked out of the country."

"Freakin' government. Won't let anybody just be."

"Dad, Maria needs someplace to stay. She needs to stay here with us. For now anyway."

He just shook his head. "No way. No way, no how. We can't get involved with any of that immigration shit. I have one son in jail. And that's one son too many."

Maria looked at me and then down at the floor. She started to stand up. It was pretty clear he didn't want her here.

"She's staying," I said. It had been a long while since I'd stood up to my father. The last time I had, he'd smacked me in the head. Hard. But I knew I had to speak up now.

My father seemed to be pretending he hadn't heard me. He set the bags of groceries on the table in front of us and began to put the milk and eggs in the old refrigerator we'd had ever since I could remember. The last item he pulled out was a cooked chicken in a clear plastic container, which he set on the table between us.

"This was on sale," he said, his voice suddenly sounding completely different. "We haven't had a good feed on chicken around here in quite a while. I hope Maria likes chicken. I really wanted some potato salad too. But you know how much they want for potato salad these days? Costs, like, an arm and a leg."

Just then Luke arrived, walking in silently like he usually did, always seeming to know just when there was food on the table. He nodded to Maria and then gave me a puzzled look, but he didn't say anything as he sat down at the table.

My father placed four of our old cracked plates on the table and took a jar of pickles out of the fridge. He grabbed a half-empty bag of potato chips from the counter. "Let's eat while it's still warm."

So we ate. The chips were stale and the pickles had been in the fridge for months. But the chicken was warm, and it was good. We ate the whole thing.

Maria was the first one to speak. "I'll do the dishes," she said.

"I'd appreciate that," my father said with the faintest hint of a smile. "Nobody around here likes to wash dishes, especially my lazy son." It was definitely just like my father to put me down in one way or another. But this time he said it like he was joking. He watched Maria as she stood up and picked up our plates. "I guess if you're willing to do some chores," he said, "you can stay for a while until things get sorted out. But just until things get sorted out."

Chapter Fourteen

Maria and I spent the evening in my bedroom, where she told me again what had happened that day and how she hid on the fire escape and then watched as her parents were put into the back of a van and driven away.

"I felt like I lost everything," she said. "And there was nothing I could do about it. I was afraid to stay there in the apartment because I thought if they found out about me, they'd come back for me too. So I just went walking around the streets. Then I ran into Oscar. He walked me here. Some other people in your apartment building started to give him a hard time, so he had to leave. But nobody bothered me."

"I'm glad you came here," I said.

"I had no place else to go."

I told Maria how Mr. Lotz had gone into the detention center. She cried a little when I told her he'd confirmed that they were definitely there, but no one was allowed to visit them.

I gave Maria the room Luke and I slept in, and I slept on the couch in the living room. Luke slept on the floor beside me. "This is great," he said. "Feels just like camping." Weird, since neither of us had ever gone camping.

In the morning my dad cooked us some eggs but didn't eat anything himself. He just drank two cups of black coffee from a big mug and said he was going out for a walk.

"You know I have to go be with them," Maria told me after a long, awkward silence.

"Okay, but we should talk to Mr. Lotz first," I said. "He was going to do some digging and find out what can be done."

It took a bit of persuading to get Maria to go with me back to school. I wasn't even sure it was the right thing to do. If the immigration people knew about her, it would be the easiest place to find her. But I had no other plan. "I'm gonna watch out for you, Maria. If those goons show up, we're gonna run."

"Where are we going to run to?"

"I don't know. We'll figure that out later."

But there were no goons waiting for us at school. Leo and Toe saw us walking in together and Toe said, "Look what the cat dragged in." I wanted to give him the finger and tell him to bugger off, but I didn't.

Before classes started we went straight to Mr. Lotz. He was thrilled to see Maria.

"You found her," he said.

"She found me."

"Either way, I'm relieved," he said. Turning to Maria, he added, "Maria, I'm so sorry."

"Thank you," she said. I wondered when I would see her smile again.

Kids were starting to file into the classroom, so Mr. Lotz led us back out into the hall. "Okay, so I did get to speak to an old college buddy of mine who now practices law. He says this sort of thing is happening all over. The bad news is, he doubts he or anyone else can stop the deportation. Maria's parents can appeal, but they'd have to do it from outside the country."

"And that's not going to help," I said.

"I know," Lotz said. "It doesn't look good."

"But he also said Maria's situation might be different because she was born here. However, she shouldn't come forward if the authorities don't already know about her. And I don't think they do…unless her parents told them."

Maria shook her head. "I know my parents. They wouldn't have said anything. They'd want me to stay here and not go back with them. They talked about that often. They kept saying it didn't matter what happened to them as long as I could stay here and find a better life. But I need to talk to them."

"I know. My friend the lawyer said they wouldn't let you in, and even if they did, they'd probably lock you up too. But I think we can call your parents, and you can talk to them."

"Really?" Maria said. "Please, let's do that."

"Okay," Mr. Lotz said. "Let's go to the office."

Maria suddenly looked suspicious. Lotz started walking toward the office, but she didn't move.

"It's okay," I said. "We can trust him."

I figured if I couldn't trust Lotz of Ideas, I couldn't trust anyone. And we desperately needed to trust someone.

At the office, Mr. Lotz spoke to the secretary, and she pointed to an empty room with a desk and a phone. We went in and he closed the door. "Don't tell anyone I did this, okay?"

We both nodded and then watched as he dialed a number and introduced himself as an immigration lawyer. He asked for permission to speak to Maria's parents and then was put on hold for several long, agonizing minutes.

When someone came on the line, the first thing Lotz said was, "Are you being watched right now?" And then he said, "Good. I'm going to put your daughter on the line. Don't overreact, please, or draw attention to yourself. And don't tell anyone there who you're talking to."

He handed the phone to Maria.

"Mom," Maria said, "I'm so scared. I miss you so much and want to be with you."

The room was quiet enough that I could hear a little bit of what her mother was saying. She was telling Maria not to come to them. I could tell Maria was trying to keep from crying.

Mr. Lotz nodded to me and pointed to the door. We left the room so she could have some privacy. Standing outside the room, I began to fear that Maria would decide to turn herself in and be deported with her parents. As the minutes passed, one of the other teachers brought in a couple of boys who looked like they had been fighting. They were led into Mrs. Warren's office.

When Maria walked out, she looked devastated. Mr. Lotz ushered us out of the office and into the quiet of the empty hallway. "I have to get back to my class," he said. "Let me know if you need anything."

I walked with Maria to the cafeteria, and we sat down at an empty table. No one was there but the kitchen staff, and they didn't pay any attention to us. I waited for Maria to speak.

"They're being sent out of the country tomorrow," she said. "There's nothing they can do about it. My mom insisted I stay here. I told her you've been helping me and said I can stay at your house. But none of this feels right. What if I never see them again?" She started to sob.

"You'll see them again, I promise." But those were hollow words. I didn't know the first thing about what was going on. I just knew I wanted Maria to stay and would do anything to keep her here.

We sat in silence for a while after that. I think Maria was still wrestling with what to do. I hated how I felt so powerless right then. When she broke the silence, she said, "My mom says I have to go back to the apartment and get a few things before the landlord throws our stuff out. Will you come with me?"

"Of course."

Chapter Fifteen

The door was open to Maria's apartment. It was a mess inside. Someone had been in there, ransacking the place. Maria didn't seem all that surprised. "We really didn't have much to steal," she said. I followed her into her bedroom, and she lifted an old beat-up suitcase out of the closet.

I felt kind of helpless but was more determined than ever to look out for her. She opened the suitcase on the bed and began to put her clothes into it. Some things had been knocked around by whoever had been in here. I picked up a framed photo with a cracked glass from the floor. It was a picture of her parents and Maria when she was quite young. I handed it to her and said, "I can fix this," but I knew there was a lot more that needed fixing than the cracked glass.

"I'm going to help you get through this," I said as she put an old doll into the suitcase and then looked around the room. I tried to imagine what it was like for her, leaving her home like this and not being able to be with her parents.

Maria went into her parents' bedroom and came back with a few more photographs and a couple of scarves that must have belonged to her mother. Then she closed the suitcase and tried to zip it up, but the zipper was broken. Broken suitcase. Broken life. I went into her parents' room, found a couple of belts and used them to tie the suitcase shut.

That's when I heard footsteps on the stairs and men's voices. They were headed our way. I quickly closed the door to the bedroom and listened. They entered the apartment, and someone kicked over a chair.

There was no place to hide. I was convinced that whoever they were, they were coming for Maria, and I couldn't let that happen. Maria nodded toward the window and the fire escape. I looked at the suitcase, but she shook her head no. We had to get out of there.

We slid open the window and slipped out onto the landing. I looked down. We were three flights up. We started down the rusty metal stairway and made it to the second floor, but the stairway to the street was missing. "We have to jump," I said. "We'll do it together, okay?"

Maria locked her eyes on to mine and nodded.

"One, two, three," she said and held my hand tightly as we took the plunge.

The sidewalk was broken concrete, and I felt my feet slap down hard on it before I tumbled and then rolled off to the side. Maria did the same. I looked over and saw a familiar face. Oscar. He waved for us to move toward him. Maria helped me to stand and gripped my hand tightly as we hobbled in his direction.

Oscar ushered us into a basement doorway and made us tuck down while he kept a lookout. Maria was shaking as I put my arm around her. Oscar put his finger to his lips, urging us to stay quiet.

I heard some angry voices as I looked back in the direction we'd come from.

Up above on the fire escape I saw three men. These were no government agents. They looked like a trio of thugs. Oscar gently pushed my head down, and we stayed like that for several long minutes, all three of us breathing heavily.

Finally Oscar said, "Okay, they're gone. Let's get you two out of this neighborhood."

My feet and legs still hurt from the jump, and it was even more painful standing up.

"Do you know who those guys were?" I asked Maria.

"No," she said.

"I've seen them around," Oscar offered. "Those three are definitely up to no good. One of them beat up my ol' buddy Crick one night, just for the fun of it."

"Why do you think they were in Maria's apartment?"

"I don't know," Oscar said. "It doesn't make a lot of sense. If they were going to steal something, you'd think they'd pick on somebody else."

Suddenly I felt really bad for Maria. "Your suitcase," I said. "It had your family pictures and your clothes. I should go back and get it."

"No," she said. "Leave it. Stay with me."

Oscar walked us to my home.

"Thank you, Oscar," I said.

Oscar bowed and said, "Glad I could be of service." I tried to invite him in, but he politely declined. "Have to be on my way," he said.

Chapter Sixteen

My father didn't say anything when he came home and saw Maria and I playing cards at the kitchen table. Maria had found a jar of spaghetti sauce and some pasta noodles, and both were bubbling away on the stove. My father walked over and lifted the lid on the sauce. "Smells good," he said. "And it don't smell like fish." He headed into the bathroom to wash up.

Maria and I set the table. Luke came in, his head hanging down. He was his usual silent self. As we ate, I didn't mention anything about what had happened that day. My father, opening a bottle of beer, seemed less irritated than he usually did and, out of the blue, asked Maria what her favorite baseball team was.

"I don't know," Maria said politely. "What's your favourite team?"

My father took another slug of beer and then coughed and laughed at the same time. "Well, to be honest, no one's asked me that in a long while. I used to like the Phillies, then the Giants, then the Dodgers. But I stopped having a favorite team, because whichever one I picked seemed to always end up being at the bottom of the pack."

Luke laughed at that and shook his head. My father smiled and looked at Luke and then at me. And I suddenly had this weird feeling. I realized we were sitting here having a normal meal and making small talk. And it felt like a real family for once. I think I even felt goose bumps on my neck.

After dinner my father went into his bedroom and turned on the little TV in there. He took a couple of beers with him, and I worried he'd get into one of his moods, but all I heard was him laughing. Maria being here had changed the mood in the old apartment.

Luke offered to wash the dishes while Maria and I played some more cards. But I could tell her mind was elsewhere. I knew she was thinking about her parents.

In the morning we walked together to school. I thought about cutting some classes and sneaking back to the apartment to get her suitcase with her things in it. But then I remembered those three creeps. What if they were watching the place?

When we arrived at the school, the secretary saw us walking past the office and came out. "Mrs. Warren would like to speak to you," she told Maria. Maria looked worried. I walked her inside.

Mrs. Warren was a no-nonsense woman who always had a serious look on her face. She had a reputation for being tough but fair, and, as far as principals go, she was probably as good as it gets. She waved a hand for Maria to sit down. She couldn't quite figure out why I was there too, but she didn't ask. Maria sat down and I sat beside her.

"I heard about your family," she said, sounding concerned. "These are some dark times." She paused and cleared her throat as she fiddled with a pencil from her desk. "We had some men here asking questions about you yesterday."

Maria said nothing.

Mrs. Warren cleared her throat again. "Mr. Lotz had already talked to me about your…situation. I'm so sorry about what happened to your parents."

"It's not fair," Maria said. "They weren't hurting anyone."

"I didn't give them any information. They didn't have any identification. So I told them you'd been absent for a week." Then she looked embarrassed. "I don't usually lie," she said. There was an awkward silence, then a knock on the door that startled Maria and me.

"It's okay," Mrs. Warren said. "I asked Mr. Lotz to come by."

The door opened and there was Lotz of Stories, trying to look cheerful. "Hi, Maria. Jake. I've been worried about you guys. Everything okay?"

There was no okay. Lotz read our looks.

"Maria," Lotz said, looking serious now, "I don't quite know how to tell you this, but I checked at the detention center again. Your parents have been sent out of the country."

Maria's hands balled up into fists. She closed her eyes and took a deep breath.

Mr. Lotz cleared his throat. "Do you have a place to stay?" he asked her.

I explained that she was staying with me. He and Mrs. Warren both looked concerned, but they didn't say anything. And then Mr. Lotz leaned toward Maria. "You were born here, right?"

Maria nodded.

"Do you have your birth certificate?"

"Yes," she said, her voice full of emotion.

"Will that mean she can stay?" I asked.

"I'm not sure," Lotz said. "The way things have changed, anything could happen. They could send her to be with her parents or they might make her a ward of the state."

"What does that mean?" Maria asked.

"Well, you'd go into foster care or into a group home until you turn eighteen," Lotz said. "They could send you anywhere."

"Jake," Mrs. Warren said, "are you sure Maria is going to be okay at your house?"

I wasn't sure what she was implying, but it was clear that the school principal, along with Mr. Lotz, had gone out on a limb for her already. I didn't think Mrs. Warren knew anything about my dad and his moods or my home life—I figured she was just concerned.

"I'll take care of her," I said.

Mrs. Warren took a deep breath. "All right. I hope we can do more to help. For now, I guess, you should both get to class."

We had different first classes in different parts of the building. I was nervous about letting her out of my sight. But she gave me a smile and said, "Go to class, Jake. I'll be okay. See you after school." And she walked off down the empty hall.

Chapter Seventeen

At the end of the day, I expected to meet Maria by the steps in front of the school. But she wasn't there. I waited for twenty minutes, but she didn't show. I asked Leo if he had seen her. They had an afternoon math class together.

"No, man. Didn't see your girlfriend. What's the matter, she avoiding you?

Maybe she's just tired of you and looking for a new guy."

But I knew that wasn't it. I got thinking about the conversation in the office. Something about it had scared her. Maybe her birth certificate was back in her apartment in that suitcase. But why would she have gone back without me?

Then it occurred to me that Maria *would* do something like that. She would have thought she'd caused enough grief for me already.

I felt a cold tingle of fear run down my spine. Damn. I started running. I didn't know what else to do. My lungs were aching and my right leg was still hurting from the jump from the fire escape. But I ran. As soon as I saw that damn old run-down apartment building, I knew something was wrong. The place had doom written all over it.

I raced up the stairs and into the apartment. I called out her name, but she wasn't there. The place had been trashed even more than before. Furniture was knocked over, and closet doors had been smashed. In her bedroom I looked for the suitcase, but it was gone.

I sat down in the middle of her bedroom floor and surveyed the scene. Had the immigration people staked out the building, waiting for her to return? Or was it something else? All I knew was, I had let her out of my sight and something really bad had happened. I could feel it in my bones. There were torn-up newspapers on the floor and pieces of broken furniture. Then I spotted a photograph, the one of Maria and her parents. It had been taken out of its frame, torn up into four pieces and thrown on the floor. What did that mean?

I picked up the fragments of the photo and tried to piece them back together. They were all smiling. Damn.

I pocketed the photo pieces and got up and left.

Back on the street, I went looking for Oscar. I found him not far from where he often slept and asked him if he'd seen Maria.

"No, Jacob, I haven't. But you need to look out for her. She shouldn't be down here by herself. I'm hearing rumors about bad things happening around here. And it's not just those immigration people."

"What kind of rumors?" I asked.

"It might just be talk, and it might be nothing, but those guys who were in her apartment, some people say they are part of some gang or organization or something. All I know is, they are up to no good, and you need to stay clear of them."

"Do you think Maria is in some kind of serious trouble?"

"Jacob, I don't know. And I may be all wrong. You need to find somebody who knows what's really going down around here. I only know what I see and what I hear. And people don't always tell me the truth. But I'll keep an eye out for her. You gotta find her."

As I walked off I was more fearful than ever about Maria's fate. Why had she come back here? And what had happened?

I thought about going to the police, but I really didn't have anything to go on. She had disappeared for one afternoon. Maybe it was nothing at all. And if I did go to the police and she turned up, it might set in motion her deportation or her becoming a ward of the state.

But Oscar's warning haunted me. I had to do something.

I knew if I could find Dalton's truck, I'd find Dalton. It wasn't at his parents' apartment building, so I tried McDonald's. He was just leaving when I showed up.

"Jakey, how goes it?"

"I've lost Maria," I blurted out.

"Shit," he said. "How?"

"I don't know. She left school and went to her old apartment, I think. And I think something happened there."

"They pick her up? The goons at immigration?"

"Could be, but I don't think so." And then I told him about Oscar and the rumors he'd heard. Suddenly Dalton looked very serious.

"Yeah, I heard about that. People being deported with kids left behind. Those kids left behind, teenage girls mostly, being abducted by a bunch of creeps. Doesn't get much more rotten than that."

"I don't understand," I said.

"Ever hear of the term *human trafficking*?"

I felt the blood drain out of my face. "Who would do this?"

Dalton shook his head. "I don't know who they are. Just talk, ya know. But whoever they are, they're not from around here. All I know is, they're tied in with a couple of big-time criminals who are already in the prison your brother's in. If you really think Maria is in trouble, I suggest you talk to your brother and see what he knows."

Chapter Eighteen

Back home, I rummaged through a drawer in the kitchen until I found the number of Cole's counselor at the prison. My father talked to him in order to get through to Cole. I dialed the number, not exactly sure what to say to this guy.

He picked up on the first ring. "Ron Charles here."

"Mr. Charles, this is Jake Compton, Cole Compton's brother."

There was a pause. "Hello, Jake. What can I do for you?"

"Well, I'm wondering how I could talk to Cole on the phone."

"That can be arranged. He doesn't hear much from his family. What's the special occasion?"

I wasn't about to trust some stranger. "Oh, I just miss my big brother. I just really want to talk to him."

More silence. "Sorry, I was just checking schedules. How about you call back at this number in one hour? I'm pretty sure I can get your brother on the line."

"Thank you," I said. "Thank you so much." And I hung up.

I think I just stared at the kitchen clock for the entire hour. My hands were sweating as I dialed the number again.

"Ron Charles here."

"Hey, Mr. Charles. It's me, Jake. Is my brother there?"

And then I heard his voice. "Jakey, is that you?"

"Yeah, it's me."

"Man, I haven't heard your voice in a long time. In fact, you sound different. You sound like you're all grown up. How's life?"

I didn't quite know how to ask him what I wanted to ask. I knew the counselor guy was there in the room. I wasn't sure I wanted him in on what we needed to talk about.

"Cole, listen, life is sort of not okay. I need your help but right now I need you to pretend we're like having a normal family conversation."

Another pause while Cole tried to sort this out. He laughed. "Normal? We always said there was nothing normal about our family. So yeah, things are good, right? Tell me more."

So I told him about Maria's parents. I also told him Maria was missing and that I thought she might be in real danger. "Dalton thinks these guys are working for someone who's in your prison. They have some kind of organization. Do you think you can find out what's going on? Who might have done this and where we can find them?"

There was another pause while Cole chewed this over. "I think that would be a great idea," he said, keeping the lid on what I was talking about. Then he leaned away from the phone and cheerfully said, "Ron, when could my little brother come visit me? It's been a long time since I've seen his ugly face."

"Day after tomorrow would work," I heard Ron say. "Ten AM."

"You hear that, Jakey? Can you make it?"

"Sure thing," I said. "I'll get there somehow."

"That's great, little brother. I'm looking forward to seeing you." And he hung up.

As I sat there alone in my kitchen, I felt scared. Scared for Maria and what might be happening to her. Scared for me and what I was getting myself into. I almost picked up the phone and dialled 9-1-1. I almost said to myself, *This problem is way too big for me, and I can't do anything about it.* But I'd been saying stuff like that to myself my whole life. And, living in this part of town, I'd learned to stop trusting the police a long time ago. I'd seen them turn the other way when bad stuff was happening. They might not even care if someone from an illegal family had gone missing.

And from talking to Cole, I realized I'd been wrong to shut him out of my life after he got busted. I had been so angry at him for being stupid. Now I needed him.

My father came home. He'd been drinking. I knew this was no time to tell him about Maria or get him involved. Luke and I retreated to our old bedroom as we often did on nights like this. Mostly just to stay out of the old man's way. After a few minutes, though, Dad poked his head in.

"No Maria?" he asked.

"No," I answered. I wasn't going to offer up more.

He shook his head. "Figures," he said, then snorted and left.

I skipped school the following morning and connected with Dalton. He said he'd drive me to the prison, on the outskirts of the city in the industrial park, the next day. And then we went driving around Maria's neighborhood, questioning people he thought we could trust. But no one had seen Maria. And it seemed no one really cared much.

"Let's go check out the apartment one more time," I said.

"You're the boss," Dalton said. So we drove there and he went in with me, but not before he grabbed a long screwdriver and slipped it under his belt. I guess I gave him a look. "What?" he said. "Just in case."

Inside it was all about the same. I didn't know what I'd expected. I poked around in drawers and looked in closets and found another torn-up photograph under a fallen-down bed. As I moved the bed out of the way, I saw that one of the floorboards was loose. I tried prying it with my fingers but couldn't get it out. Dalton saw me and used his screwdriver to remove it.

At first I just noticed the dust, dirt and rat poop. But then I saw it. An envelope with a piece of paper inside. Maria's birth certificate. I was pretty sure now it was why she'd left school that day and come back here. But I still didn't know what had happened after that.

Chapter Nineteen

Dalton drove me to the prison as planned. I was kind of scared. I'd never been inside a prison before. I'd never even visited Cole, not once. And now I felt almost too scared to go in. And I had assumed Dalton would go in with me, but when I started to get out of the truck, he just sat there staring at the windshield.

"You coming with me?" I asked.

He tapped the steering wheel with the palm of his hand. "What are you, crazy? I ain't goin' in there. I got this feeling that if I walked in there, they'd find some reason to not let me leave. No way. I'm not going in there."

And that was that.

So I walked up to the gate and told the guard who I was and that I was going to visit my brother. He let me through and then I went into the prison itself. I was searched and questioned and finally left sitting in an ugly waiting room with gray walls and a gray floor. I could see why Dalton was afraid of coming in here. After about ten minutes a man in a suit walked in.

"Hi, Jake. I'm Ron Charles. I'll take you to a room where you can speak with your brother."

As I walked down a long corridor, I heard voices echoing throughout the building. Angry voices. Shouting voices. I heard doors opening and closing, and everything had a cold, hard sound. I wondered if I would have to sit in a booth and speak on a phone to my brother while separated by a glass window. But it wasn't like that.

It was another gray room with a bare wooden table and two chairs. Cole was already there. He smiled as I walked in, and I suddenly felt so guilty for not staying in touch with him, for not coming to visit sooner.

Ron just kind of bowed and said, "I'll be back later." And he left.

"Jakey, man, it's good to see you. What's goin' on with your hair?"

Yeah, my hair. It had grown quite a bit since Cole had seen me last. I smiled. "I finally convinced Dad to stop giving me that crappy haircut with those damn cutters."

Cole shook his head. "I didn't think any one of us would ever win that battle. But you're lookin' good, kid. The hair. And you got bigger. And something else I can't quite pin down. But it's different in a good way." He scratched his chin and then said, "I know what it is. You look stronger."

I shook my head. "I don't feel stronger."

"How's Luke?"

"Luke's Luke. He still doesn't say much."

And that was it for the small talk. "Okay, little brother, I know this isn't about some family reunion."

I nodded. "Yeah, I'm sorry I haven't stayed in touch. I really am. But you're right. This is about Maria."

Cole took a deep breath. "Jake, it's a really shitty world out there."

"Tell me about it," I said.

"Dalton was right. There's a couple of guys inside here. We all know to stay the hell away from them. They moved down here from somewhere up north and started getting in on whatever they could—gambling, drugs. If it was illegal and they could cash in on it, they did it."

I was almost afraid to hear what he was going to say next. I leaned forward.

"So, word is, they saw an opportunity coming their way. The government was cracking down on illegal immigrants, and some of the kids—teenagers mostly—were slipping through the cracks. Either staying on with relatives or just staying behind and trying to make it on their own. That's when these guys would swoop in and kidnap them. Make them work for them or sell them."

"Sell them?"

Cole nodded. I didn't want him to explain further.

"But these two got busted for some big drug deal from a ways back. They ended up in here, but their operation kept going."

"You think they took Maria?"

"Yeah, I do. I hope not. But it sounds like their thing. Like I said, it's a really shitty world out there. And in here, it's even worse."

"I have to find her."

"I know. It took some doing, but I have an address. Basement of a house at 1532 South Street. There's three of them running the operation."

"Three," I repeated. "I think I've seen them."

"Jake, what are you gonna do?"

"I don't know yet. Think I should go to the police?"

Cole gave me a look. "Look who you're asking. The way I hear it, the police already know what's going on, but because it involves families of illegal immigrants, they just don't care. I wish to hell I was out of here so I could help."

I looked down at the table. "Me too," I said. I knew I was in way over my head. Maybe there was nothing I could do to save Maria. I felt helpless.

"Jakey, look at me."

I looked him straight in the eye.

"Talk to Pop. Tell him everything."

"Are you crazy? He's always telling me to run from trouble. To stay out of it. Whatever *it* is."

Cole leaned back in his chair. "You're going to have to tell somebody."

Ron was back in the room now. We stood up. Cole gave me a big bear hug and said, "I'm gonna be out of here in eighteen months. We've got some catching up to do."

Chapter Twenty

Dalton was tapping his fingers nervously on the steering wheel when I got in the truck. I told him what Cole had said. "That is definitely some nasty shit," he said. "What are you gonna do?"

"I'm going to find Maria," I said. "No matter what it takes."

Dalton fired up the engine and put the truck in gear. "Count me out. I've seen those dudes."

He didn't say much more as we headed toward our part of town. When we were back in the neighborhood, I asked him if he'd drive around to Duskie and see if we could find Oscar.

"Why Oscar?" he asked.

I didn't answer.

After going up and down a couple of streets, we found Oscar with his shopping cart. "Thanks, Dalton," I said and got out.

Oscar was glad to see me, but his look changed when I told him what I'd learned about Maria. I told him the street number.

"I know that old house," he said. "Not good people. I've been through their trash. Booze. Needles. Magazines. Curtains always closed. I never see

anyone around there in the daytime."
And then he asked me the same thing
Dalton had. "What are you going to
do?"

"I don't know," I said. And I didn't.

Oscar walked me home. We didn't
talk. The streets seemed noisier than
usual. And more unfriendly. When we
got to my building, Oscar leaned toward
me. "You need my help, all you have to
do is ask." Then he lightly tapped me
once on my forehead and rolled his cart
away.

Luke was in the bedroom with head-
phones on, listening to music. He looked
up and nodded when I walked in. I lay
down on my bed and closed my eyes.
All I could think about was Maria.

A while later I heard the front door
open. I knew my father was headed for
the kitchen. He had already grabbed a

beer when I sat down at the table across from him.

"Rough day?" I asked.

"Aren't they all?"

"I saw Cole today," I said.

My father looked at me in shock. "You visited him?"

I nodded. "I think he's doing okay. He says he might be out in eighteen months."

"Eighteen months can be a long time."

"I told him about this problem I have."

"Problem?"

"Yeah. He told me I should talk to you about it."

"That don't sound much like Cole. He never talked to me about what he was up to."

"Well, maybe he's changed."

My father took a sip of his beer. "Tell me about this problem."

So I filled him in, about Maria and about what Cole had revealed to me.

He was listening, but he stared at his beer bottle the whole time. When I'd finished he set it down on the table. "That's one hell of a problem, Jake. Sounds like somebody better do something about it."

He was breathing real heavy, the way he did sometimes when he was about to freak out. He got up from the table and kicked the chair over, then walked into his bedroom and slammed the door.

I sat there in disbelief. It looked like Cole had it all wrong. The story had made my dad angry, but then, hell, everything made the old man angry. So now he had shut himself in his bedroom. Yeah, I figured, that was the father I knew and loved. Cole so totally had it wrong.

But after a few minutes the door opened. My dad walked back into the kitchen and looked right at me.

He was holding a gun. One of those small handguns like I'd seen a couple of kids carrying at school. He set it down on the table.

"You own a gun?" I asked. "You always told us you hated guns."

"I do. I hate guns. But I have this one." He slid it across the table to me. I couldn't believe this was happening. That gun scared the shit out of me just sitting there on the table. My father had always been unpredictable. And he'd flare into violence over the smallest thing. This was not a man who should own a gun.

He looked at the gun and then at me. It was like he was reading my mind. "Don't worry. I don't have any bullets. If I'd had bullets, I would have killed someone a long time ago."

Neither of us noticed that Luke had come out of our bedroom. "What's goin' on?" he asked, standing right behind us.

I was sure my father was going to tell him nothing, but instead he pointed to the gun and explained why it was sitting on the table.

No one spoke at first.

Then Luke just nodded and said, "I'm coming with you."

My father gave him a hard look and then said one word. "Good."

Then he walked over to the sink, bent down and opened a cupboard door. He pulled out a crowbar and set it on the table as well. "Always have backup. That's rule number one." He studied the gun and the crowbar for a minute and then said, "But we need to know exactly what we're getting into before we go charging in there. I can't say I've done anything like this before. So you have to let me sleep on it."

I wanted to say we needed to go over there right away. But I kept quiet. As I went to bed that night, I was pretty certain my father would change his mind by morning. Maybe his wanting to help was just the beer talking. I'd seen that plenty of times before.

Luke looked up from the martial-arts magazine he was reading in bed. "We really gonna do this?"

I thought maybe he was getting cold feet. "You don't have to be part of it," I said. "It's not really your problem."

"No, Jakey. You don't get it. I feel like I've been waiting to do something like this all my life."

Chapter Twenty-One

But we never did get that good night's sleep. None of us. At around eleven thirty there was banging on our door. This had happened before. Usually it was one of the drunk neighbors coming to see if we had any beer left in the fridge. Or coming to cuss out my father for being the mean son of a bitch he usually seemed to be.

I got up first. Through the peephole I could see it was Oscar. That was truly strange. I opened the door and let him in just as my father stumbled into the kitchen.

"Jacob," Oscar said. "I've been watching that place ever since you told me about it. I've seen four of them in there today. Those three big guys and a young skinny punk not much bigger than you. So here's the thing. Those three guys you saw, they left. I could be wrong, but I think it's just the kid who's left there now with whoever they're holding."

My father was blinking, standing there in his boxer shorts, staring at Oscar. He looked pretty pathetic, really, and not at all happy about being woken up. Luke was in the room now too, looking like an oversized cartoon character in his too-small pajamas.

"Let's do it," my father said, heading

back to his bedroom. I assumed to put some clothes on.

"Yeah, let's do it," Luke said, like he'd done this sort of thing a million times before.

Me, I was scared. But the wheels were in motion, and I knew there was no turning back.

"How'd you get here, Oscar?"

"Dalton. He's downstairs in his truck."

I dressed as quickly as I could. I tucked my pocketknife into my pants pocket. Then I grabbed my old baseball bat from the dust under my bed. Louisville Slugger. Solid oak, not like the metal ones. From the one summer I had played baseball for three weeks before I got kicked off the team.

My dad got in the front of the truck with Dalton. Oscar, Luke and I sat in the back. Charging through the dark city streets was like some kind of a wild dream. I could feel the adrenaline kicking in and my heart pounding.

I could hear Luke's running shoes tapping on the floorboards in a nervous, quick beat. Oscar touched him on the knee and then placed his forefinger on my forehead. "Stay cool. Stay focused. I have a feeling this is going to be one of those truly interesting nights."

Interesting didn't quite seem like the right word.

Before I could think another thought, Dalton was bringing the Ford to a stop in front of the building Oscar had scoped out earlier. The upstairs was dark. So was the downstairs. Windows all boarded up. My father got out of the front of the truck, crowbar in one hand and gun in the other.

Yeah, it was going to be an interesting night. And my family—well, for once I felt damn good about my family.

I pointed to the basement door. We really didn't have a clue what was behind there.

Oscar, Luke and I followed my dad up the broken cement walkway and stood there in the dark metal doorway. My father tucked the empty gun into his belt and was about to use the crowbar to pry open the door when Luke stopped him.

"Wait," my brother said. And in one powerful motion, he kicked hard on the door. Once, then twice. It swung open.

My father was the first one in, and Luke was right on his heels. The only light in the room was coming from a computer screen. I ran my palm down the wall until I found a switch and flicked it on just in time to see a young guy charging at my father with a knife thrust out in front of him. My father just stood his ground, ready to defend himself with the crowbar, but my brother charged forward, kicked the knife out of the guy's hand and then delivered a powerful kick to his stomach. The creep toppled forward and fell to the floor.

Luke pushed him down flat and then kneeled on his back, putting all his weight to good use.

I looked around the room. Empty bottles, trash, old pizza boxes. But no Maria. There were two doors off this main room, both locked. I thought I could hear muffled cries, but it could have been anything. My heart was beating loudly.

My father pried open the first door. Inside were two frightened teenage girls. They stumbled out into the room, their mouths taped and their hands locked behind them with plastic zip ties. I took

my pocketknife and cut the plastic off
one girl and then the other, but before I
could help them with the tape over their
mouths, one of them pushed me away
and they both ran. In an instant they
were gone.

I dropped my baseball bat, grabbed
the crowbar and started to pry open
the second door. Then I noticed it had
some heavy kind of bar across it that
wouldn't budge. It was held in place
by a padlock. A couple of good smacks
with the curved end of the crowbar, and
the lock broke free. I pushed on the
door, not knowing what was going to be
on the other side.

Inside was Maria. I couldn't get the
door completely open, but I could reach
in and touch her. I shoved at the door
with my shoulder and tugged her out of
that horrible black hole. She was bound
too. I carefully cut the plastic until her
hands were free.

Watching this all play out, Luke must have lost his focus, because the guy on the floor somehow toppled Luke and got up. My father tried to grab him, but he weaved out of his way and headed for the doorway. Oscar tried to stop him but got shoved onto the floor.

"Let him go," my father said. "And let's get the hell out of here."

Luke and I helped Maria into the front of the truck, which Dalton had kept running. I carefully removed the tape from over her mouth as Oscar, my father and Luke piled into the back of the truck. We looked around for the other girls, but they were nowhere in sight.

Maria took a deep breath, sobbed, but said nothing as we sped through the night.

Chapter Twenty-Two

It's safe to say none of us slept much that night. Maria and I sat in my bedroom and talked.

"I went back for my birth certificate," she said. "That's when they found me."

I opened a drawer, took out the envelope and handed it to her. "I went there first looking for you. I knew something was wrong."

"You found it!" she said, taking it from me. "Thank you. You know, I'm not sure I want to stay here in the city anymore. I don't feel safe. I think I should go find my parents."

"I'll help you do that if you want," I said, although I felt sad already at the thought of losing Maria again.

"But there's something I have to do first."

"What's that?" I asked.

"I need to go to the police and tell them everything I know about those men. If I don't, they'll keep doing what they're doing."

She was right, of course. But I still wasn't sure I trusted the police.

Maria rubbed her wrists where they had been tied together with the plastic zip tie. She lifted her sleeves, and I could see the bruises on her arms as well. "Jake, all my life I've expected bad things to happen. And they usually did.

My parents were always afraid they would be caught."

She paused and looked up at me. I saw something different in her face. She wasn't scared anymore.

"While I was trapped in that room, I started to believe this had happened to me because I was a bad person."

"You've never been a bad person!"

"I think I know that now. But I've always felt like a victim. I'm not going to be a victim anymore. And I need to do something to help other girls like me."

I understood all too well what she meant. She and I had tried to fly under the radar at school. Tried to stay invisible. We'd watched out for each other, but we'd never gotten involved when anyone else was in trouble.

"All right," I said, smiling. "Everything changes tonight."

"Everything," she said, smiling right back at me.

Chapter Twenty-Three

My father was already up and cooking eggs when we walked into the kitchen. It wasn't like him to make breakfast for anyone, including himself. Luke was sitting at the kitchen table, dressed for school like it was an ordinary day.

My father nodded to the chairs at the table, and we sat down with Luke as the eggs were slipped onto plates and set in front of us. Toast popped up from the toaster and was promptly delivered to us in a kind of dance. This wasn't like my father at all.

"So?" he said, leaning against the kitchen counter as we began to eat.

I was about to say, *So what?* but Maria spoke first.

"I'm going to talk to the police. Tell them everything."

He looked at Maria. "Your idea?"

"Yes," she said. She didn't have to say any more. "Somebody has to stop them. They could ruin the lives of a lot of people."

"You want me to go with you?" he asked.

"Maybe," she said.

"But first we're gonna talk to Mr. Lotz, the teacher at school who tried to help us before," I added. "He's got a lawyer friend. It might get complicated, but I don't care."

"Complicated is right," my dad said. And I almost thought he was going to try to talk us out of it. But he didn't. "Eat up," he said. "You got a big day ahead of you."

My dad walked us to school. He was worried that the goons might come looking for us.

Maria, me, Luke and my dad—all walking down the street together like a family. My dad still had his gun with him, tucked under his coat. I had my pocketknife in my pocket. Luke had his martial-arts skills that he'd been working on for years. And he also had a newfound confidence. You could see it in the way he walked. The only things missing were the crowbar and the baseball bat.

No, the only thing really missing was Cole. I missed my brother and decided I was going to stay in touch with him.

I was going to be there to help him when he got out as well.

"They'll be looking for me at work," my dad said as we arrived at the school. "Call me at the Shit Shack if you need me."

We went in quickly and went straight to Mr. Lotz's room. School hadn't started yet, and he was sitting at his desk, grading some papers. He lit up when we walked in the room.

Maria told him her story. Our story.

I think his jaw kind of dropped and just stayed there. "You're not making this up, are you?"

"No," Maria said. "It's all true."

"And you want to go to the police?"

"We want you to help us," I said. "You and your lawyer friend."

He blinked once, twice, and looked confused. I almost thought he was going to turn us down. He swallowed hard and said, "Okay. I will."

Then he made a call to Mrs. Warren and asked for someone to take over his morning classes again. He phoned his lawyer friend and did his best to explain the situation, ending it by saying, "We need to do this now. This morning."

I think his friend must have tried to put him off, because Mr. Lotz looked a little ticked. "Derrick. Remember that time back in college?"

There was a brief pause, during which this Derrick dude must have remembered whatever had happened back in college. Apparently, he owed Jim Lotz a favor. And lucky for us, this was it.

Then there was a cab ride to an office downtown, where we were introduced to the lawyer. He seemed pretty unhappy about getting involved. Nonetheless, he reluctantly agreed to go with us to the police station.

After a fifteen-minute wait we were ushered into a room with a female officer.

The lawyer spoke for us at first and began by saying that Maria's parents had been deported. The officer tried to brush us off at first. "I think this is a matter for immigration, not the local police."

"Maria was born here," I said. "She's a citizen. I think you should hear the rest of the story."

Maria's voice was kind of shaky at first, but as she began to tell the officer what had happened to her, she became more animated, more assertive. I listened and watched as she looked the officer in the eye and said what needed to be said.

Something slowly changed. The officer's eyes grew wide, and she said nothing at first.

She turned to her computer and started to type on the keyboard. "You got an address?"

"Yeah—1532 South Street," I said.

She turned back to Maria. "You willing to file a complaint? Willing to testify in court?"

"Yes," Maria said.

"Where are the other two girls who were with you?"

"I don't know," Maria answered.

"Would you try to help us find them?"

"Of course."

"Where are you living now?"

"She's living with me," I said.

"Are you family?"

"She's my cousin," I lied.

"I'll need to talk to your parents."

"You can call my father," I said. "He works at the Fish Shack on Henry Street."

She nodded.

It did get a bit complicated after that. We spent most of the day in the police station. Mr. Lotz and the lawyer stayed with us. And my father was called in. I'd already called him to give him a heads-up that Maria was now part of the family.

At the police station my dad was back to being his old belligerent self. He just couldn't help it around the cops. When asked about his relationship to Maria, he blurted out, "I'm her uncle, goddamn it. You think I'd be down here wasting my time if she wasn't family?"

Things didn't exactly work out as we hoped. Before the day was out, someone higher up in the police department insisted that Maria "go into protection" until the kidnappers were brought in. It was for her own safety, they said. And none of us could argue against that.

Chapter Twenty-Four

I didn't see Maria at all after that for what seemed like a really long time. I knew the cops had nabbed the three creeps, but they hadn't gone to trial yet. I'd go down to the police station where they knew me now and talk to that police officer, who I now knew as Jill. Jill told me Maria was fine and being looked after, that I'd be the first to hear when it was safe.

I talked to Cole a couple of times a week, thanks to Ron Charles. I worried that news of Cole's involvement—his snitching—would get around in prison and someone would try to punish him for it.

"Don't worry about me, Jakey. I'm holding my own here. I'm just glad I could help out. You gonna let me meet this Maria sometime?"

"You bet," I said. Cole sounded a whole lot more positive now than he had when he lived at home. I'm not going to say prison did him good. But he was changed.

In fact, I guess a lot of things changed after the night we rescued Maria. My father quit his job at the Fish Shack. Yep. Just walked in a couple of days later and quit. Walked down the street to the Royal Diner and asked if they had work. He got hired that day.

It's not exactly a four-star restaurant, but it was a step up in the world.

Dalton started to get more steady work cleaning out people's attics and basements and hauling their junk away. Oscar worked with him some days, and occasionally they did the bottle roundup together, carrying the goods across town to avoid Dirty Dave. I tagged along some days just for the hell of it.

Kids at school found out about Maria and what had gone down, and about Luke busting the door down and sitting on that guy. Suddenly he had some respect around the neighborhood, and he seemed to like that just fine.

Mr. Lotz took me aside after class one day and asked, "You remember that word I asked you to look up?"

I had pretty well forgotten all about it. "Self-something," I said.

"*Self-actualization*," he said. "Big word. Big idea."

That was Lotz of Ideas for ya.

"Well, I think it worked."

"What worked?"

"You did. You found the thing you are good at."

I wanted to ask him exactly what he meant, but kids were already piling into the room. I decided to let it go.

About a month after we'd found Maria I heard on the news that those three men who had been arrested had now been convicted of human trafficking. The police had even made the connection to the boss that was in Cole's prison. I knew this was all good news, but I was beginning to wonder if I'd ever see Maria again.

I went back to the police station to ask about her, but Jill said she wasn't allowed to tell me anything about Maria. Not yet.

And then, a couple of days later as I was walking out of the school one sunny afternoon, there she was. Waiting for me.

She gave me a big hug and said, "I'll never forget what you did for me."

"No problem," I said and probably blushed. "You gonna come stay with us?"

She shook her head. "No, they know now we aren't related. It was nice of your dad to cover for me like that though. I'm going to stay with a foster family. They're really okay. I've got my own room and everything. One of the other kids there is a real jerk, but I'm learning how to deal with him. I guess I'm okay there for now. But I'll come visit you. And you can come over whenever you want."

"That's cool. I will. What about your parents?"

"My foster parents figured out a way that I can talk to them on Skype every day. I can't believe my parents can use Skype. But they go down to the public library every day at a certain time, and we talk. They really want me to stay here."

"Are you scared?" I asked. "After what happened?"

"Yeah, I think about that sometimes. I still have nightmares. But I feel stronger now—like I can do things. Like I can help make things happen."

Now she was smiling. Looking me straight in the eye, not hiding behind her long dark hair.

"Besides," she said. "I can always call in the team if things go bad."

"They're not going to go bad," I said.

"Yeah, I think I know that now." We walked off to find Oscar and see what he'd have to say about how things were gonna turn out.

Lesley Choyce is the award-winning author of dozens of books for young adults, including *Kryptonite* and *Identify* in the Orca Soundings series. He has been shortlisted for the Stephen Leacock Medal, the White Pine Award, the Hackmatack Award and the Governor General's Award. For more information, visit lesleychoyce.com.

PREVIEW OF KRYPTONITE

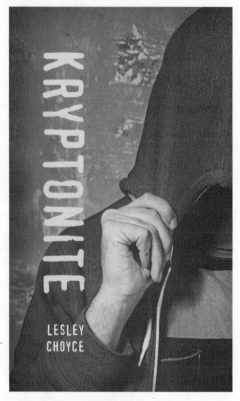

KRYPTONITE

LESLEY
CHOYCE

9781459816565 PB
9781459816572 PDF
9781459816589 EPUB

Chapter One

Mr. Carmichael, my high-school philosophy teacher, held my essay in his hands and just shook his head. "Jackson, I can't believe you plagiarized an essay on plagiarism."

"I think that's an unfair accusation," I snapped back.

We were sitting in the staff room, just the two of us. He glared at me for the third time since we had sat down. Then he slapped the essay down on the table and started typing away on the keys of the laptop in front of him. Without looking up at me, he continued, "I asked you to write this because you had plagiarized twice already. Your first essay, you simply printed off the Internet."

"I regret that," I said. "I really do." What he said was true. I had been sloppy.

"The second essay, you paid one of your classmates to write for you."

"I just asked Davis for some help on it." Well, actually I had conned him into doing it for me. Davis was smart when it came to school stuff but stupid when it came to most everything else. I didn't know how Carmichael had found out. Most teachers wouldn't have bothered investigating.

"But this, Jackson, this was your masterpiece," Carmichael said, turning the laptop screen toward me so I could see it.

I leaned forward and tried to focus on the screen.

"The highlighted parts are the ones you copied. Underneath each, you'll see the sources I tracked down."

Very little of the essay was not highlighted. And he had found every chunk I had cobbled together from various Internet sources. It must have taken him hours.

"I apologize. I guess I forgot to document those sources. I spent a lot of time doing research for this essay. I was trying to prove to you that I could be a good writer."

"Bullshit," he blurted out.

I kept my cool even though I could see Carmichael was losing his. I knew I was in a tough spot. But hey, it was only an essay. I tried to look hurt.

"Jackson, why didn't you just write the damn essay yourself?"

I blinked and pretended to be confused. "I don't know. I just thought…" I let my words trail off. The truth is, I'd thought I could outsmart this guy because he was just a high-school English and philosophy teacher. But he had nailed me good.

"There's a word for you, mister."

Carmichael closed the laptop and wrung his hands. I didn't know why this plagiarism thing had pissed him off so much. I was thinking he might actually hit me. In fact, I was hoping he would. I could definitely work with that.

I looked him in the eye defiantly. "Go ahead and say it."

He stared at me for a second and then ripped my paper into pieces and threw them in my face. Then he picked up the laptop and left, slamming the door behind him.

But he didn't say it. He didn't say the word. I was left wondering if he had really found out.

Titles in the Series

orca soundings

Knifepoint
Alex Van Tol

Kryptonite
Lesley Choyce

Last Ride
Laura Langston

Learning Seventeen
Brooke Carter

Learning to Fly
Paul Yee

Lockdown
Diane Tullson

Masked
Norah McClintock

Middle Row
Sylvia Olsen

My Side
Norah McClintock

My Time as Caz Hazard
Tanya Lloyd Kyi

Night Terrors
Sean Rodman

No More Pranks
Monique Polak

No Problem
Dayle Campbell Gaetz

Off the Grid
Lesley Choyce

One More Step
Sheree Fitch

One Way
Norah McClintock

Outback
Robin Stevenson

Overdrive
Eric Walters

Pain & Wastings
Carrie Mac

Picture This
Norah McClintock

Pinch Me
Gabrielle Prendergast

Plastic
Sarah N. Harvey

Rat
Lesley Choyce

Reaction
Lesley Choyce

Redline
Alex Van Tol

Refuge Cove
Lesley Choyce

Responsible
Darlene Ryan

Riley Park
Diane Tullson

Riot Act
Diane Tullson

River Traffic
Martha Brack Martin

Rock Star
Adrian Chamberlain

Running the Risk
Lesley Choyce